Just Look Just Look Just
Just Look JUST LOOK Loo
Just Look JUST LOOK
Just Look Just Look Just Loo
Just JUST LOOK Just Look
Look JUST LOOK JUST LOOK
JUST LOOK Just Look Just
Just Look Just Look Just
Just Look JUST LOOK JUST

TANA HOBAN

JUST LOOK

 GREENWILLOW BOOKS, NEW YORK

The full-color photographs were
reproduced from 35-mm slides.

Printed in Singapore by
Tien Wah Press
First Edition 10 9 8 7 6 5 4 3 2 1

Library of Congress
Cataloging-in-Publication Data

Hoban, Tana.
Just look / by Tana Hoban.
      p.   cm.
Summary: The reader views
photographs of familiar objects,
first through cut-out holes, then
in their entirety.
ISBN 0-688-14040-8 (trade).
ISBN 0-688-14041-6 (lib. bdg.)
1. Toy and movable books —
Specimens. [1. Visual perception.
2. Toy and movable books.]
I. Title.   PZ7.H638Ju   1996
[E]—dc20   95-10233   CIP   AC

JUST FOR MAX

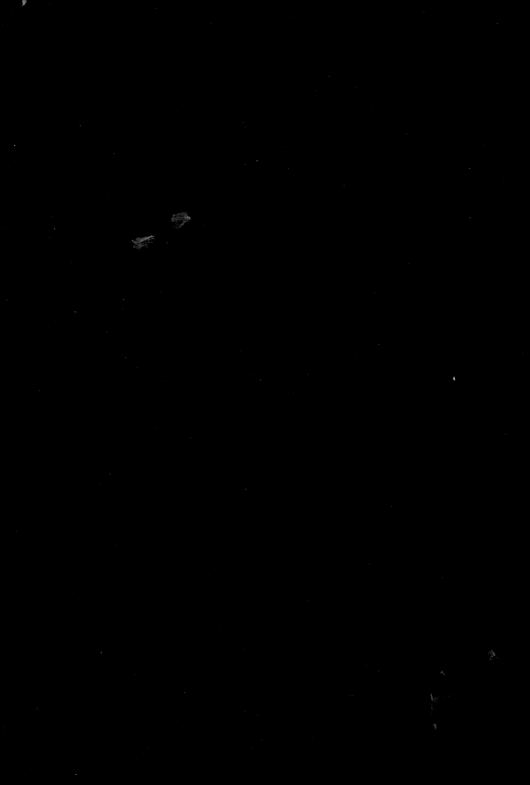

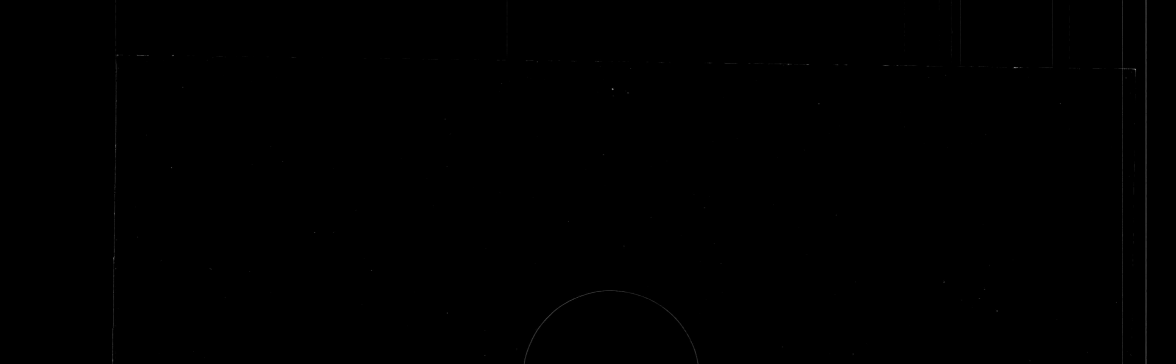

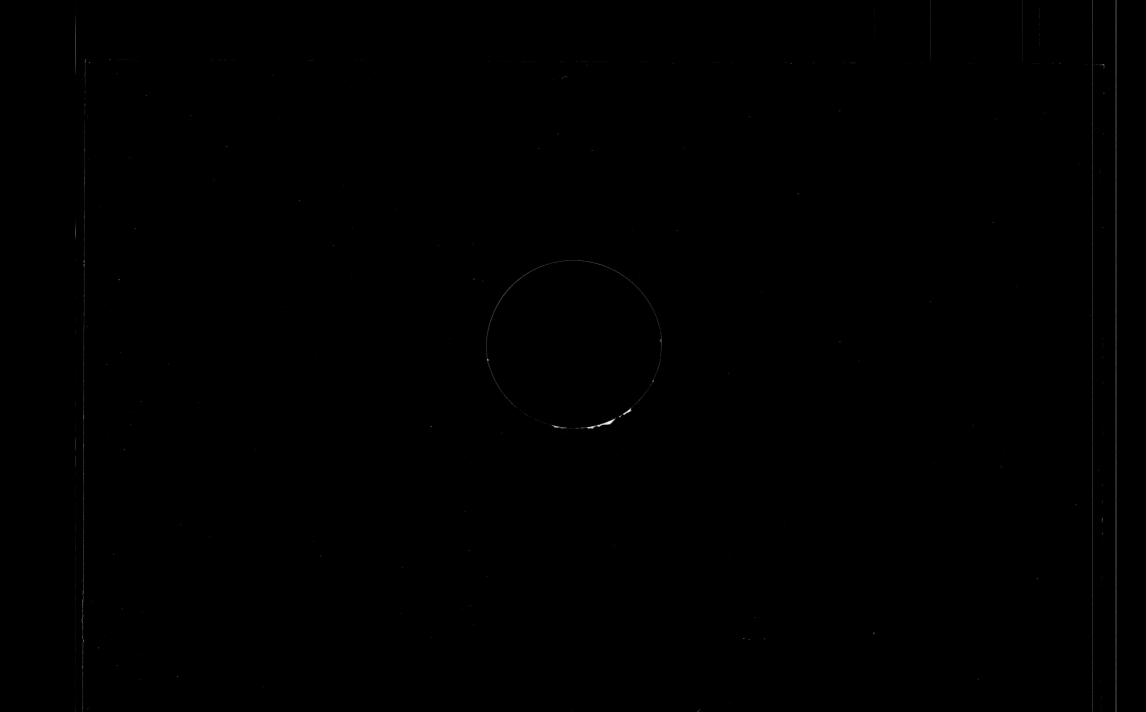

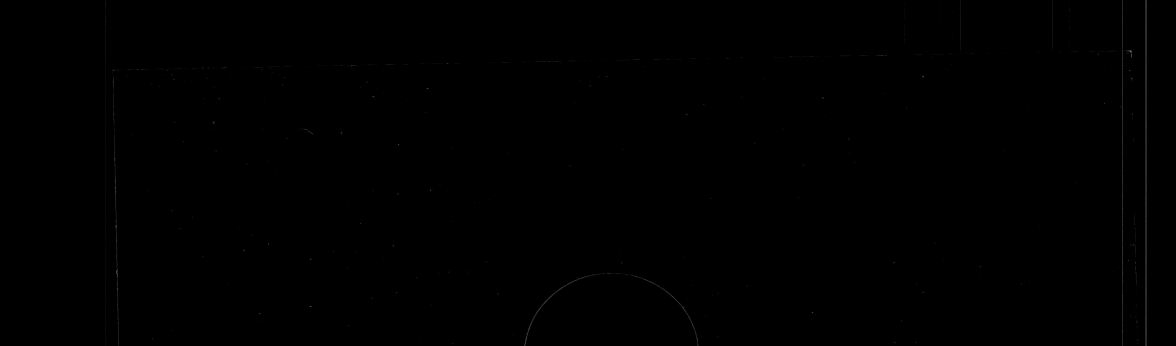

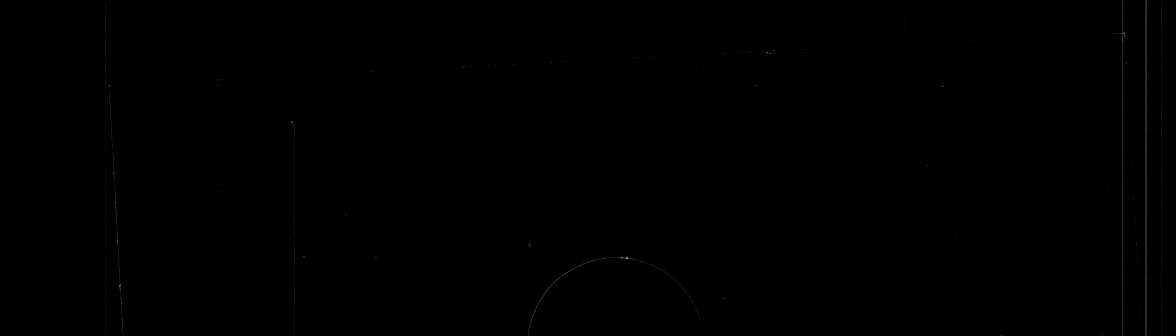

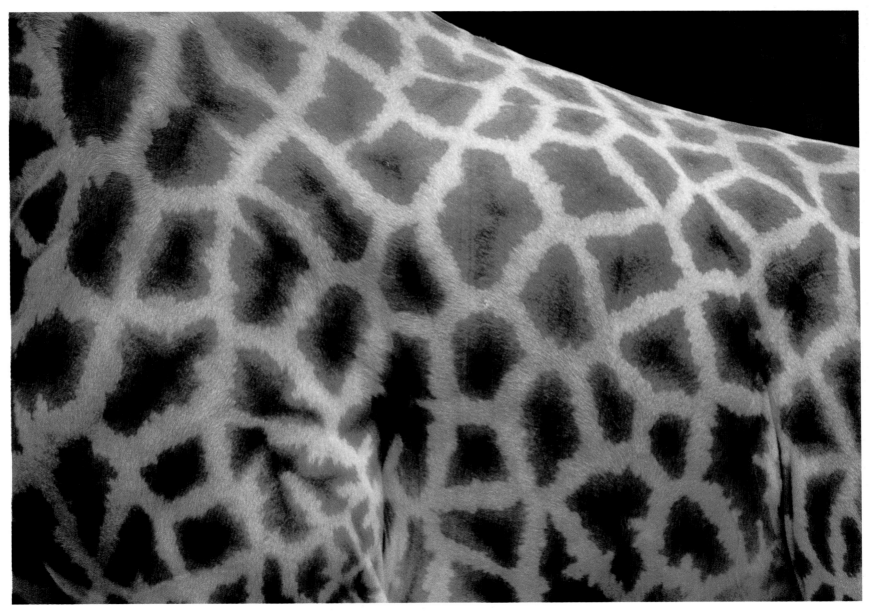

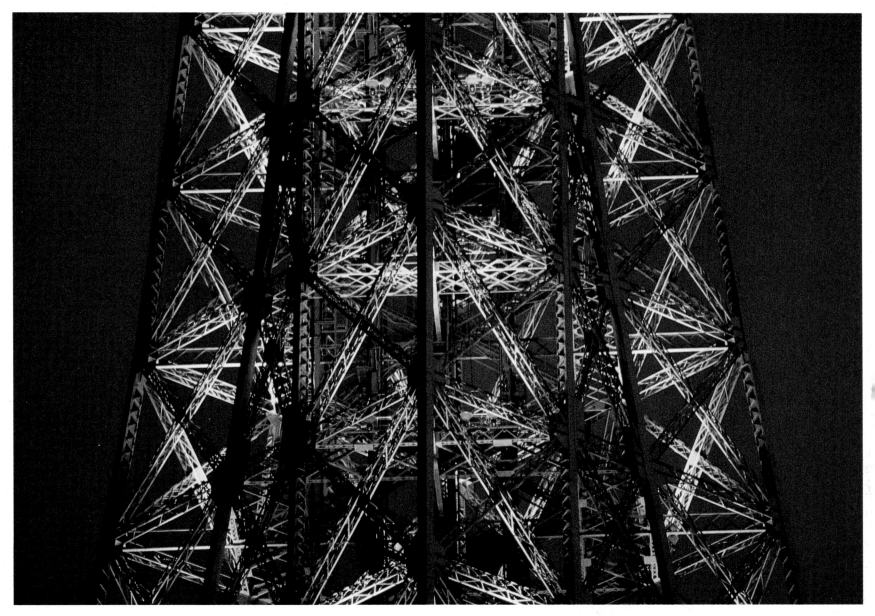

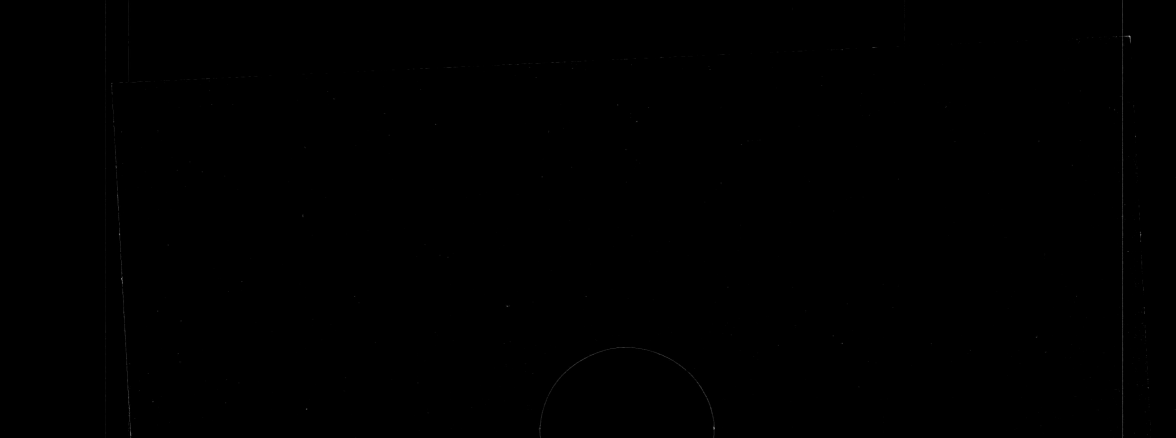

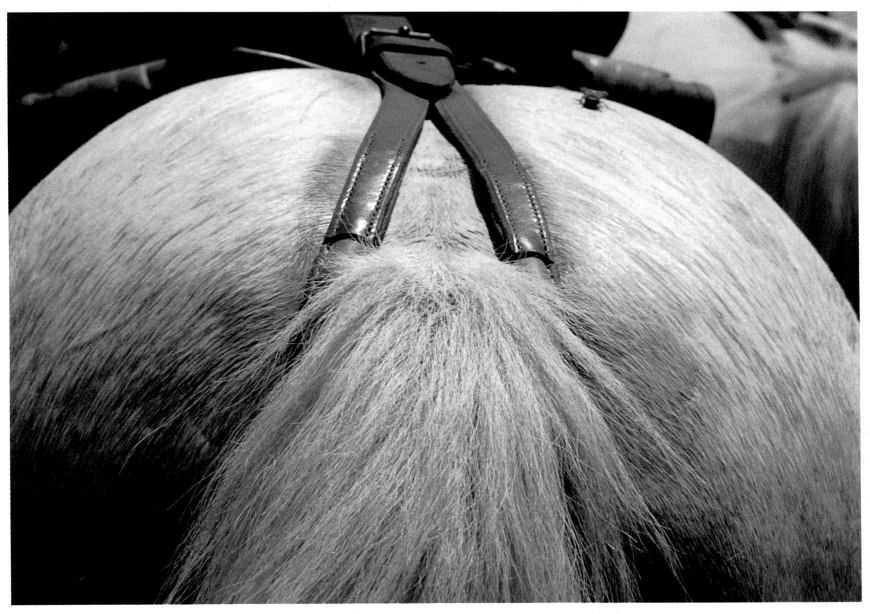